LE RENARD ARGENTÉ

THE SILVER FOX AT WAR

AMANDA SMITH

ISBN: 9781693922060

PREFACE

There are a few certainties in life: death, taxes, and Chase Utley staring down a pitch as it hurtles toward his body.

On May 19, 2017, I saw a photo of Chase Utley going nose-to-chest with a towering Giancarlo Stanton during a Marlins/Dodgers brawl and thought "Chase Utley isn't afraid of pain because he fought in World War II." I still have no idea why that was my first thought, but it was, and the idea amused me immensely. Like so many of the things I do on Twitter, I decided to run the joke into the ground.

Seriously, I don't know why anyone follows me.

For the next two seasons, Chase continued to be the grizzled veteran, and I continued to write weird little vignettes about a thoroughly fictional soldier fighting for the US army in World War II. Sergeant Utley is not Chase, but I would like to think that if they ever met in real life, Sgt. Utley would give Chase Utley an "atta boy, Sam" for his focus, his discipline, and his complete disregard for personal safety.

If you're reading this, thank you for buying the book. If you're reading this and you're associated with the Dodgers, Major League Baseball, or Chase Utley, please don't sue me.

"Got the name from a group of Maquisards hiding in a farmhouse south of Nîmes. They called me Le Renard Argenté because I brought them a fresh chicken and the belt buckles of the Nazis I'd killed."

"You think I'm scared, little boy? I was in France. Just me and six Nazis, a little town outside Luxembourg. Ran out of bullets. Used my hands."

"**H**it me.
   I need that pain to feel alive. I spent three weeks alone in a foxhole in Nuremberg. Stabbed myself in the thigh to smell the blood."

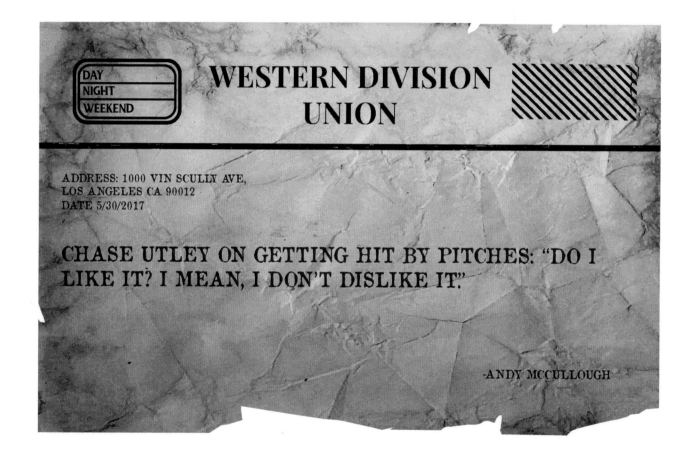

WESTERN DIVISION UNION

DAY
NIGHT
WEEKEND

ADDRESS: 1000 VIN SCULLY AVE,
LOS ANGELES CA 90012
DATE 5/30/2017

CHASE UTLEY ON GETTING HIT BY PITCHES: "DO I LIKE IT? I MEAN, I DON'T DISLIKE IT."

-ANDY MCCULLOUGH

"**P**ain takes me back. Strasbourg, 1944. The SS captain had six rounds in his gun. When it was over, I had two in my leg and his heart in my hand."

"I remember my 1000th kill. Morocco. I was tracking a Nazi spy to his rendezvous. The SS officer's blood was rich, vibrant red. Like a fez."

"Peeling bananas takes me back to Guam. I hid in a banana tree for three weeks. Made traps from the peels.

They slid to their deaths."

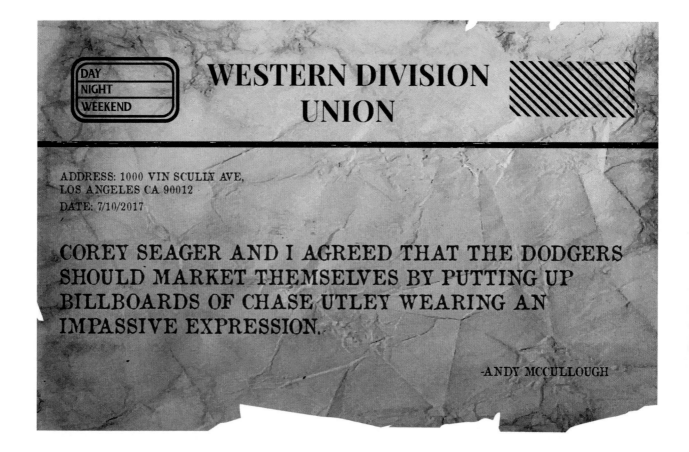

DAY
NIGHT
WEEKEND

WESTERN DIVISION UNION

ADDRESS: 1000 VIN SCULLY AVE,
LOS ANGELES CA 90012
DATE: 7/10/2017

COREY SEAGER AND I AGREED THAT THE DODGERS
SHOULD MARKET THEMSELVES BY PUTTING UP
BILLBOARDS OF CHASE UTLEY WEARING AN
IMPASSIVE EXPRESSION.

-ANDY MCCULLOUGH

"Watch the games. Don't watch them. I don't care. I once killed 4 Nazis using only a map of Brussels."

"Joy. I knew it once. A small bar in Rive Gauche. Her name was Evangeline. I left her to return to the war. We never spoke again."

"**I** was cornered by Wehrmacht in Dresden. I fought my way out. Never ran. But when Posey's behind the plate, I can run."

"Feel the adrenaline.
The power. It'll save your life
when you're 200km from your troops
armed with only a pen knife."

"Good stuff, Rook. Took it like a man. Reminds me of when Fritz thought a cheek full of shrapnel could stop me.

It didn't."

Chase knew slumps. In Köln, he didn't kill any Nazis for three days. On the fourth day, he took out two with one bullet.

"I call all the greenies Sam. I'll learn their names when they hand me ten Nazi scalps.

And 100 street tacos."

"**I** had a perfect game once. Went up against 27 Nazis and didn't let any of them walk. So I know what it means to a man."

Chase smiled. All day, the number had eluded him, but finally he remembered: he had skinned nine Nazis in Paris.

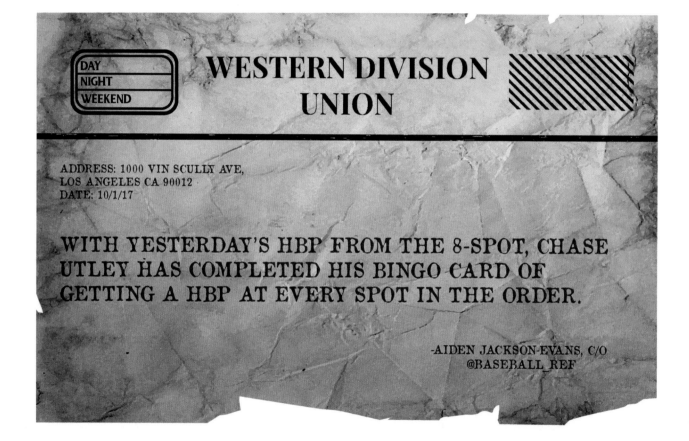

DAY
NIGHT
WEEKEND

WESTERN DIVISION UNION

ADDRESS: 1000 VIN SCULLY AVE,
LOS ANGELES CA 90012
DATE: 10/1/17

WITH YESTERDAY'S HBP FROM THE 8-SPOT, CHASE UTLEY HAS COMPLETED HIS BINGO CARD OF GETTING A HBP AT EVERY SPOT IN THE ORDER.

-AIDEN JACKSON-EVANS, C/O
@BASEBALL_REF

Chase grimaced as his fist connected, but he felt no pain. This was it. He had finally fought a Nazi in all eighteen French regions.

Lineup Spot	HBP
Batting 1st	15
Batting 2nd	27
Batting 3rd	131
Batting 4th	6
Batting 5th	4
Batting 6th	7
Batting 7th	7
Batting 8th	2
Batting 9th	5

Chase looked around the dugout. He'd been here before. 1943, pinned down near Tours, outnumbered two to one.

They survived. They had to.

"That's it, Sam. Take the hit.
Feel the pain in your arm.
Draw it into your heart.
Feel your heart grow stronger.
Then strike."

"I climbed the ladder, just like when I climbed into the commander's window. Slit his throat.

You could say I robbed him of a hit."

Chase wiggled his toes. He hadn't felt them since the sleet started six hours ago. He had been in position for ten.

Then he saw it—a dim flicker, a candle on the icebox cake Ma made.

One, two, three down the line.

His shot rang out and the flame dropped.

Happy birthday to him.

Chase looked to his right. An angle of the jaw, the shrug of a shoulder—in those moments, he saw the resemblance.

She had been a member of the French Resistance. He had begged her to escape to America when she told him she was pregnant.

Chase had secured passage for her within days. They fought viciously—how could he be so selfish to expect her to abandon her country?

For years he replayed the fight, the words he said. When he came to her flat the next day, all trace of her was gone. He wondered if she escaped or was caught. If she kept the child or lost it.

But now, standing next to his young teammate, with his familiar grimace and her effortless grace, Chase knew.

Chase couldn't remember what toothpaste tasted like. It had been so long. Four months into tracking top Nazi brass through Germany and he had run out. His next resupply would be in Nîmes, in two months. He flossed with the sinews of the men he killed.

WESTERN DIVISION UNION

DAY
NIGHT
WEEKEND

ADDRESS: 1000 VIN SCULLY AVE,
LOS ANGELES CA 90012
DATE: 1/22/18

Chase Utley is a free agent. He's also working out with a group of Dodgers at Dodger Stadium, for those wondering if a return might happen.

- Ken Gurnick

Chase was not the bright-eyed boy who'd left the corn fields of Long Beach. There was something wild in him now—or maybe it had always been there, long before the beaches of Normandy. He took his orders from Uncle Sam, but at heart, he was a free agent.

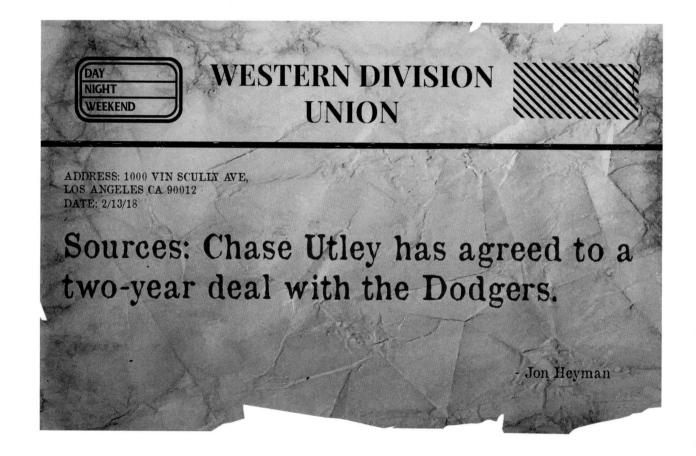

DAY
NIGHT
WEEKEND

WESTERN DIVISION UNION

ADDRESS: 1000 VIN SCULLY AVE,
LOS ANGELES CA 90012
DATE: 2/13/18

Sources: Chase Utley has agreed to a two-year deal with the Dodgers.

- Jon Heyman

Chase tried to remember what life was like before he had stormed the beaches of Normandy, before he had lain awake in the sleet near Kraków, but it was like trying to remember a dream just as you blink awake. When Uncle Sam asked for two more years, how could he say no?

The shrapnel in his knee shifted slightly as he knelt. The remains of the mortar didn't hurt anymore—the scar tissue had done its job—but it brought Chase back to that bright morning near Vichy when he knelt over the captive Abwehr officer and sharpened his blade.

"**I** wear the sunglasses so they can't see my eyes. Don't know where I'm looking. Don't know when I'll strike. Don't know if I've been hit.

They say the eyes are the window to the soul. There's no place for a soul in war."

"**D**oesn't matter how good your eye is. You stay sharp. You stay focused. You get lazy, that's when Fritz gets you and then you'll be lucky if they put you in a cage."

"I know it was a lucky hit. But that's the thing about war. They're all lucky hits. I wasn't the best soldier. Didn't have the cleanest shots. Couldn't track worth a damn. But I was lucky.

And that's the only reason any of us came home."

"The smell reminds me of the sewers of Paris. The Vichy held the city, but the world below the streets was mine. For months I crawled, a rat in a maze, looking for the cheese at the end. Only for me, the cube of cheddar was the shock on the Wehrmacht officer's face before I shot him."

"The hardest part of war isn't the killing, or the fear, or the pain. The hardest part is knowing when you save someone and have to leave them behind. I've spent my whole life wondering if strangers I rescued grew old. It's an honor to serve with you."

"**I** never collected trophies or souvenirs. Just scars and the shrapnel in my knee. I didn't need proof. I know what I've survived. But one day, my son's gonna show his son this ball. He'll say 'My old man took every bullet the Nazis fired at him. Never dodged a hit.'"

"Disappointment. Failure. I was stationed outside of Cannes. I had a fully loaded sniper rifle and the SS officer in my sights. Then I sneezed.

I've never forgiven myself."

"It's an old injury. The fog makes it bark. I was planting explosives behind an officer encampment. A Scharführer ducked out for a smoke. Couldn't risk using my gun, couldn't get to my knife, so I used my hands. Tore out his tongue and my ligament."

WESTERN DIVISION UNION

ADDRESS: 1000 VIN SCULLY AVE,
LOS ANGELES CA 90012
DATE: 5/9/18

NOMAR GARCIAPARRA: HE ALREADY KNOWS THE SCOUTING REPORT. HE KNOWS HOW STRONG EACH AND EVERY ONE OF THE OUTFIELDER'S ARMS ARE OUT THERE, AND WHETHER OR NOT HE CAN TAKE THE EXTRA BASE.

JOE DAVIS: LET'S BE HONEST, CHASE UTLEY KNOWS THEIR CHILDREN'S NAMES. HE KNOWS WHAT TOWNS THEY'RE FROM.

"I know their children's names. I know what towns they're from. I know what they had for dinner and what they fear when they lie awake in the dark. You have to know everything about your enemy if you want to know the hour they're going to die."

Chase watched Logan fumble and grimaced. Chase liked Logan. He was a good kid—a family man, salt of the earth. But his glove had more holes in it than the SS officer Chase faced in a shadowy alley in Opole.

"Enemy territory. Dunkirk, France. The mission: let myself be captured. They marched me through the camp to the Generaloberst. I took the guttural jeers and tried not to smile. I knew my hands would be slick with their blood before the lights came on for the night."

"**I** know that when Doc puts me in I'm just cannon fodder. Nothing new for me. In war, it doesn't matter how good you are with a gun, how fast you are with your knife. Every time you go into battle, you're just trying to put your body between the enemy and their target."

Chase listened to the rookies trade stories and shook his head, remembering the last thing his father told him. "Chase, if you're really good at something, you don't have to tell them. You let them tell you with their dying breath."

"**Y**ou do the things I've done, you don't expect to be acknowledged. No one back home knows about the nights I spent hiding in pig shit on a farm in Nîmes. They don't know about the time my gun jammed and I had to use my bootlace for a garrote. They see me, they thank me for my service, but they don't know what they're thanking me for. It took me years to learn how to reply—to lower my head, tip my hat, and let them thank me. They don't know what I've done, but they know I did it because they couldn't."

Chase watched from the dugout. He'd trained his men to take a hit, to sacrifice their bodies for a win. The bowstring tension within him lessened slightly. He'd taught them all he could. His job was done.

    "Atta boy, Sam."

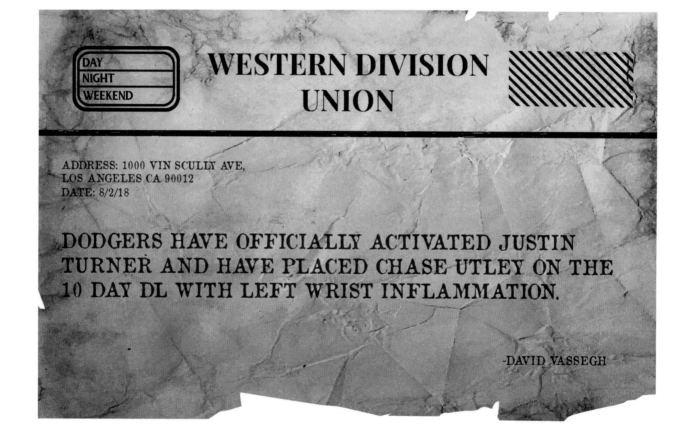

"Ten clicks east of Vienna. I knew I was being tracked but I didn't double-back. Figured I'd let him come to me. Sprained my wrist when I snapped his neck. Sometimes it acts up."

"**B**efore you get your first kill, you lie awake wondering how you want to die. Growing up, I'd heard my old man's friends talk about mustard gas. Only part of war they never laughed about. And I bet it's still not as toxic as what comes out of Kersh."

"Ten clicks from Kielce. Rations ran out and I wasn't getting a resupply till after the mission. I set squirrel traps and ate the meat raw. When you're that hungry, you don't put your food down long enough to cook it. Wouldn't have put it down for God or Satan."

"Joy. Victory. The blood running hot through your veins and sticky on your skin. You don't know if your head's buzzing from the altitude or the adrenaline. All you know is the heat of the Sergente maggiore's blood as it melts the snow under his body."

"**I**'ve had a pretty unique career, when I look back on it. Enlisted at eighteen, selected for a special ops team. Spent the next three years in German-occupied territories killing SS officers.

But they don't make bobbleheads of you clutching a man's still-beating heart."

"For me, I've always played the game the right way. I never killed an unarmed man who didn't deserve it. Let the honorable ones die an honorable death. I woke up every day grateful, and every morning I swore to myself that I'd kill more Nazis than I did the day before."

"Chase's son Benjamin is six, his son Max is three. They're getting old enough that they ask why sometimes they wake up at four a.m. and Chase is sitting awake in the hallway, cleaning his old Colt, staring at the front door."
– Joe Davis

"Poznań. Lying in the mud. Cold. Bleeding from a hole in my side, thinking of the corn fields back home in Long Beach. Knowing this was the end. Then I heard it. I thought it was just my heart struggling to beat. But it was the anthem.

    I stood up."

WESTERN DIVISION UNION

ADDRESS: 1000 VIN SCULLY AVE,
LOS ANGELES CA 90012
DATE: 9/29/18

So I captured Utley giving this bat to Joc
Pederson before the game. Pederson
proceeded to hit a leadoff HR with it!

- Alanna Rizzo

"**S**ometimes a man has to make his own weapons. Whittled this on the road to Burgundy. Used it to take down an SS officer. He thought he could start over, open his own vineyard. His blood stained the bat like red wine on a new carpet."

"**S**ometimes you get a hit. Sometimes you don't. What matters is that you show up early, play hard, and never let the Nazis win."

"Is it cold, kid? Does it burn? Let it burn. Everyone says that war is full of pain, but it's the victory that hurts the most. You wipe the blood from your face. You pull your body out of the mud. And you reload your weapon, because there's always another war."

WESTERN DIVISION UNION

ADDRESS: 1000 VIN SCULLY AVE,
LOS ANGELES CA 90012
DATE: 9/30/17

MANNY MACHADO REVEALED DURING THE SPORTSNETLA
COVERAGE OF THE CLUBHOUSE CELEBRATION THAT A
PLAYER TOLD HIM HE SHOULD'VE HUSTLED ON THOSE
DOUBLES HE THOUGHT WERE HOME RUNS. WHO DELIVERED
THE MESSAGE? CHASE UTLEY, OF COURSE.

-MATTHEW MORENO

"You always run it out. Made that mistake a few times when I was a rook, too. Thought I killed an Obersoldat with a single shot. Started to walk away, he winged me with his Luger. Learned the hard way: always hustle, always check for a pulse."

WESTERN DIVISION UNION

ADDRESS: 1000 VIN SCULLY AVE,
LOS ANGELES CA 90012
DATE: 10/28/18

IT MIGHT BE THE LAST DAY OF HIS CAREER. AND HE'S NOT EVEN ON THIS DODGERS ROSTER. BUT CHASE UTLEY IS STILL TAKING GROUND BALLS IN BP.

BECAUSE OF COURSE HE IS!

-JAYSON STARK

"They want you to get soft. Lose your instincts. But when you're lying in bed and you hear a boot creeping over the creaky top step, it's those instincts that'll keep you alive."

War is endless, until it ends. Chase goes home. He folds up his uniform. He lives his life. Gets a job, kisses his wife, raises his boys.

Has a beer, tells stories, laughs about the time he fed an SS officer's tongue to a pig he'd befriended in Karpacz.

Sometimes he wonders if he's still a soldier. If it's still as instinctive as the pulse in his veins, or if it escaped his body like a man's dying breath.

Time passes and an old friend reaches out. They met after Buchenwald was liberated.

There are still evil men, Sol says. They must be brought to justice. Help us find them.

That night Chase pulls his Colt out of the old hatbox. A restlessness Chase didn't know he felt settles, a cat stretching in the sun.

"I always wanted to see Argentina."

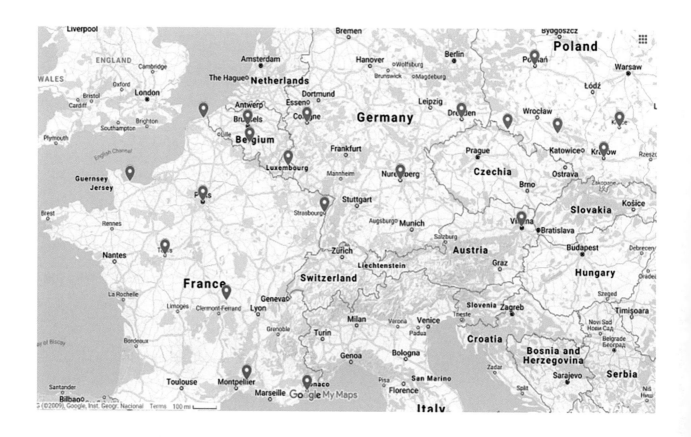

"Latest I've ever shown up to boot camp. Get ready, grunts."

ACKNOWLEDGMENTS

This book would not have been possible without the friendship and support of the incredible Dodgers twitter community, in particular my coven of Vin Scully Avenue witches. Thank you to everyone who encouraged my narcissism by asking repeatedly if I'd ever turn the #WW2Utley tweets into a book, and for the subsequent enthusiasm when I announced a book would exist—this absolutely would not have happened without you.

Thank you to AJ Gonzalez, Todd Munson, Randi Radcliffe, Rebekah Shibley, and Jess for providing images of their Chase Utley bobbleheads for pages 64 and 65. A special thank you to Jess for providing additional reference photos for the artwork.

And of course, thank you to the 2017 and 2018 Los Angeles Dodgers, as well as the associated broadcast team and reporters. Those were two of the most fun seasons I've ever experienced as a fan. To me, this book is very much a scrapbook of those seasons.

INDEX OF ARTWORK

Kendall Caroline Avery   31, 32, 33, 34

Paul Briggs   16, 43

Bill Bushman   6, 11, 20, 28, 39, 44, 47, 52, 62, 76, 78, 80, 82

Ang Choi   8, 9, 12, 19, 22, 26, 30, 40, 41, 48, 53, 55, 57, 60, 61, 66, 67, 69

Claudia L. Letonja   cover artwork

Rebecca Mills   13, 15, 17, 18, 23, 27, 35, 37, 42, 46, 49, 54, 56, 70, 71, 85

ABOUT THE AUTHOR

 Amanda Smith is a third generation Dodgers fan and Angeleno. A graduate of Tisch School of the Arts' Dramatic Writing program, she has put her BFA to good use by tweeting extensively with a half-finished screenplay open in another window. You can follow her on Twitter at @amandartubbs.